EDWARD

Based on *The Railway Series* by the Rev. W. Awdry

Illustrations by
Robin Davies and Jerry Smith

EGMONT

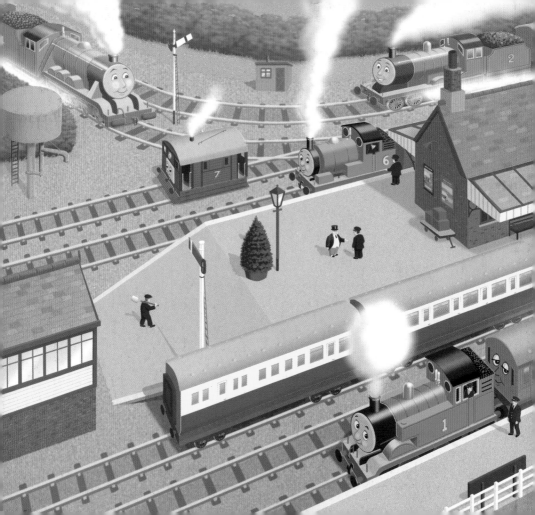

EGMONT

We bring stories to life

This edition published in Great Britain in 2007
by Egmont UK Limited,
239 Kensington High Street, London W8 6SA
All Rights Reserved.

HiT entertainment

1 3 5 7 9 10 8 6 4 2
Printed in China

TO THE TRAINS ⟶

This is a story about Edward the Blue Engine. As an older engine, he could be noisy and rather slow. The big engines called him names, but Edward soon had the chance to prove there was more to him than 'Old Iron'…

Edward was getting old. His parts were worn and the big engines called him 'Old Iron' because he clanked as he worked.

One day, he was taking some empty cattle trucks to the market.

"Come on! Come on! Come on!" puffed Edward, as he clanked along the line.

"Oh! Oh! Oh!" screamed the rattling trucks.

Some cows were grazing in a field by the line. When Edward clattered past, the noise and smoke upset them. They twitched their tails and ran!

The cows charged across the field! They broke through the fence, and crashed into the last few trucks! A coupling rod broke and half the trucks were left behind!

Edward felt the trucks jerk suddenly. But he thought they were being naughty as usual.

"Those Troublesome Trucks!" he cried. "Why can't they come quietly?"

Edward had reached the next station before he realised what had happened.

News of the accident quickly reached the other engines.

"Silly Old Iron! Fancy allowing cows to break his train!" laughed Gordon. "They wouldn't dare do that to me. I'd show them!" he boasted.

Edward pretended not to mind. But Toby was cross.

"Don't worry, Edward," he said. "Gordon's very mean to call you names. He doesn't know what he's talking about, cows can be very troublesome!"

This made Edward feel a little better.

A few days later, Gordon rushed through Edward's station.

"Mind the cows!" he laughed, as he roared along the line. But his Driver could see something on the bridge ahead.

"Slow down, Gordon!" he said, and shut off the steam.

"Pah!" said Gordon. "It's only a cow! Shoo!" he hissed, moving slowly on to the bridge. But the cow wouldn't 'shoo'. She had lost her calf, and felt lonely.

Gordon stopped. "Be off!" he hissed. But the cow kept walking towards him and mooed even louder! Gordon was scared and backed slowly away.

His Driver and Fireman tried to send the cow away. But she wouldn't move. The Guard told the Porter at the nearest station.

"That must be Bluebell," said the Porter. "Her calf is here. We'll bring it to her, now."

"Moo!" bellowed Bluebell when she saw her calf. And she nuzzled her happily.

Gordon was very quiet on his way back to the station. He hoped no one had heard about Bluebell. But the story soon spread.

"Well, well, well!" chuckled Edward. "A big engine like you, afraid of a little cow!"

"I wasn't afraid," huffed Gordon. "I didn't want the poor thing to hurt herself by running into me."

"Yes, Gordon," said Edward, solemnly. But he knew the real reason why Gordon had stopped!

A few days later, Edward was late with the passengers for James' train.

"It's Old Iron again," grumbled James. "Edward always keeps us waiting."

Thomas and Percy were annoyed. "Old Iron!" they snorted. "Why, Edward could beat you in a race any day!"

"Really!" huffed James. "I should like to see him do it."

Edward heard James as he pulled into the station, but he just smiled.

Later that week, James' Driver felt unwell. His Fireman was ringing for a relief Driver when he heard the Signalman shout.

James was puffing away without a Driver! His Fireman ran after him, but James was going too fast! The Signalman had to halt the other trains to make sure there wasn't an accident.

"Two boys were standing on James' footplate!" explained the Signalman when James' Fireman returned. "Edward is bringing the Inspector. He needs a pole, and a coil of wire rope."

James' Fireman was waiting with the pole and rope when Edward arrived.

"Good man," said the Inspector. "Jump in."

"Don't worry, we'll catch him," puffed Edward.

By now, James was very frightened. He had realised that he didn't have a Driver.

"I can't stop," he wailed. "Help! Help!"

"We're coming," cried Edward. And he puffed with every ounce of steam he had, until he was level with James' buffer beam.

The Inspector carefully climbed out of Edward's cab and stood on his front. He had made a noose out of the rope and tied it to the end of the pole. He was trying to slip it over James' buffer! The engines swayed and lurched and the Inspector nearly fell, but he saved himself just in time!

At last, he did it. "Got him!" he shouted, and pulled the noose tight around James' buffer. Then he carefully climbed back into Edward's cab.

Edward's Driver braked gently, so he didn't snap the rope. And James' Fireman scrambled across and took control of James.

Edward and James puffed back side by side.

"So 'Old Iron' caught you after all!" chuckled Edward.

"I'm sorry," whispered James. "Thank you for saving me. You were splendid."

When they reached the station, The Fat Controller was waiting.

"That was a fine piece of work," he said. "I'm proud of you, Edward. You shall go to the Works, and have your worn parts mended."

"Oh! Thank you, Sir!" said Edward, happily. "It will be lovely not to clank any more."

James' Driver soon got better and went back to work. The naughty boys had got such a shock when James started moving that they decided to wait until they were much older before trying to drive a train again.

When Edward came home, he felt like a new engine! James and all the other engines gave him a tremendous welcome. Even Gordon let out a cheer! Edward was very happy that he would never be called 'Old Iron' again!